To all my family and friends who encourage and support my creativity.
I love you all dearly.

Printed and bound in China
First Printing 2018
ISBN 978-1-7328246-0-7

Share your gratitude with us on social media!
#thankfulfrankie

www.kathleencruger.com

THANKFUL FRANKIE

By Kathleen Cruger

Illustrated by Al Johnson & Emily Serruto

Frankie was a kid full of life and fun,
who swam in the sea and soaked in the sun.

Frankie loved the parks, the sliding and swinging,
the skipping, hopscotching, dancing, and singing.

But what Frankie loved most was all of the toys!
The ones that stood still and the ones that made noise.

The puzzles, the games, the blocks, and the balls.
Big ones, little ones —Frankie wanted them all!

Frankie had many toys all kept in a pack,
which hung rather heavy behind Frankie's back.

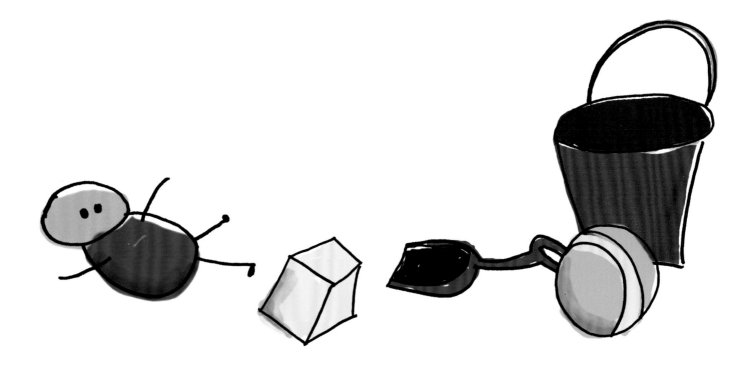

One day Frankie woke with energy to run!
Frankie looked out at the sun and thought, *how fun!*

Frankie tied up his shoes and ate a quick snack,
and set off for the park with the giant toy pack.

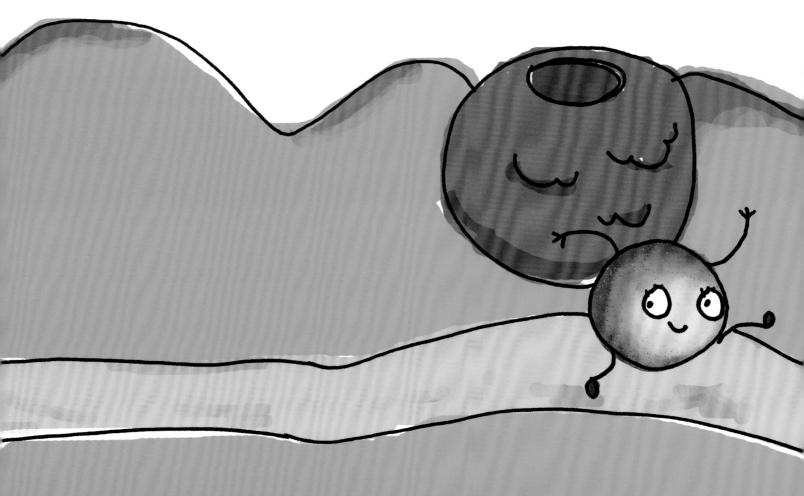

"Frankie! Frankie! We're having a relay race!
We need your quick speed to help us win first place."

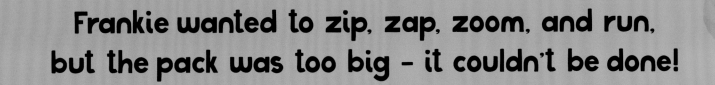

Frankie wanted to zip, zap, zoom, and run,
but the pack was too big – it couldn't be done!

Frankie thought for a moment, then took off the pack.
Frankie felt light as air and ran twice 'round the track!

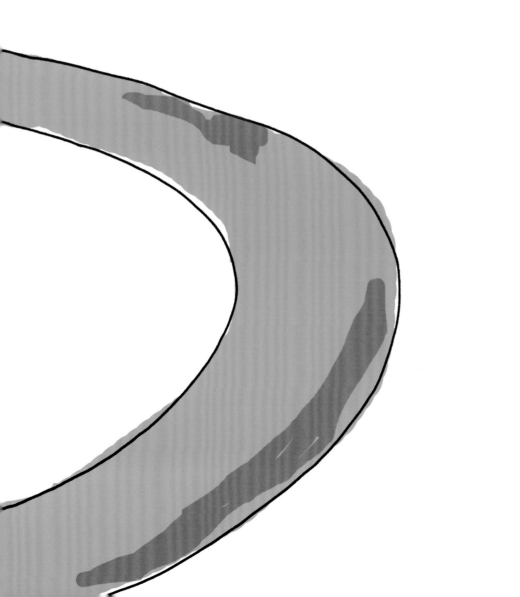

"Did you have a good day?" Frankie's parents asked.
"My day was incredible, I had a blast!"

"And your big pack full of toys? Where did it go?"
Frankie thought for a moment, then shouted, "OH NO!"

"My pack of toys! I left them all at the park!"
Frankie couldn't go now—it was after dark.

Frankie ran to the bed and began to cry.
"My dolls and my blocks and my planes that can fly!"

"I'm so sad!" Frankie screeched and cried a bit more,
until Frankie heard a soft knock at the door.

"Don't worry Frankie, it will be okay.
You don't need toys to be happy, anyway!"

"Happiness doesn't come from toys or doo-dads.
It comes from family, friends, and fun you've had."

"You can make a short list each and every night
of all the joy-filled things you have in your life."

"Try it right now, give it a go, and you'll see
you don't need blocks, balls, or boats to be happy!"

Through the tears Frankie began listing away
all the wonderful things that happen each day.

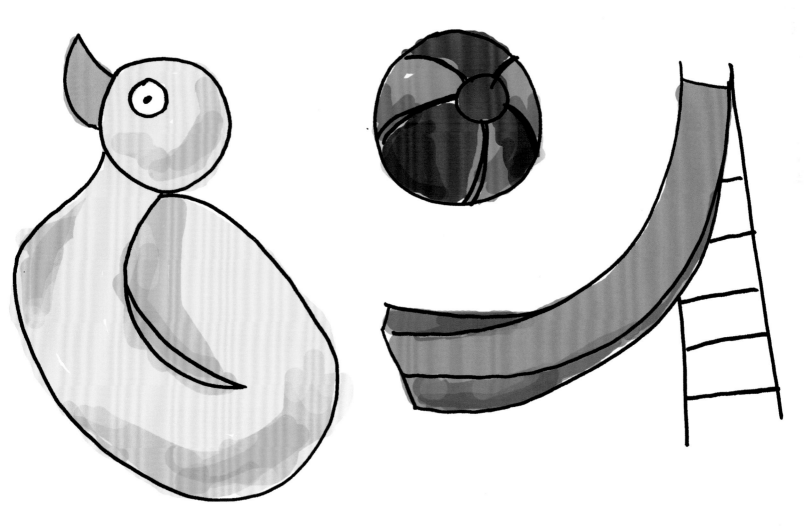

"I'm thankful for my family and all that they do.
They feed me, they hug me, and teach me things, too!"

"I'm thankful for my friends who are always kind
and my teachers at school who help all the time."

"My cozy warm bed, the food that I eat,
the clothes that I wear, the shoes on my feet!"

"The sun that shines bright and the breeze that blows by,
the rain that rains down and the trees that grow high."

Frankie woke the next day with a heart full of joy,
forgetting all about the lost pack of toys.

WOW! Frankie thought, *My life is truly the best!*
I am so very thankful, grateful and blessed!

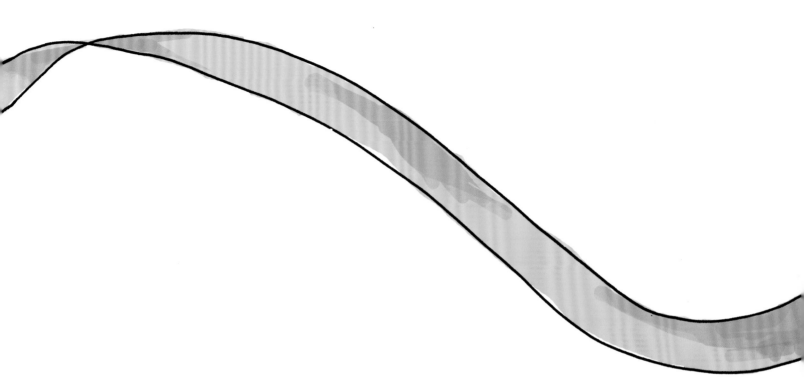

So Frankie continued each and every night
listing all the things that brought smiles and light.

Each year Frankie grew, the list grew much longer,
as practicing thanks makes happiness stronger.

Life was much better, for when Frankie felt sad,
the list showed Frankie that life wasn't so bad.

Now it's your turn to try! What makes your life great?
Take a moment each day to list off some thanks!

Life won't always be easy—some days it's tough,
but your list lets you know there's always enough.

NAME SOMETHING THAT MAKES YOU HAPPY!

WHAT MAKES YOU SMILE?

WHAT IS YOUR FAVORITE THING IN NATURE?

NAME SOMETHING THAT MAKES YOU LAUGH!

WHO ARE YOU THANKFUL FOR?

WHAT DO YOU LOVE ABOUT YOUR FAMILY?

TAKE THE THANKFUL FRANKIE SECRET GRATITUDE CHALLENGE!

Let someone know you are thankful for them! Write a short note, bake a sweet treat, draw a pretty picture, pass along a copy of *Thankful Frankie*, or create something special. Secretly drop off their note or gift and wait for the power of gratitude to make their day!

Share your challenge with us:
@thankfulfrankie   #thankfulfrankiechallenge

WE CAN'T WAIT TO SEE WHAT GOOD YOU DO!